Chameleons

Hetty the Yeti

Written and illustrated by
Dee Shulman

A & C Black • London

To Chris

JS
_____
i 4515 78

First published 2003 by
A & C Black Publishers Ltd
37 Soho Square, London, W1D 3QZ

www.acblack.com

Copyright © 2003 Dee Shulman

The right of Dee Shulman to be identified as the author and
illustrator of this work respectively has been asserted by her
in accordance with the Copyrights, Designs and Patents Act 1988.

ISBN 0-7136-6435-5

A CIP catalogue for this book is available from the British Library.

A&C Black uses paper produced with elemental chlorine-free
pulp, harvested from managed sustained forests.

Printed and bound in Singapore by Tien Wah Press (Pte) Ltd

Chapter One

Hetty the Yeti lived in a Yeti-shack with her Yeti-Mum, her Yeti-Dad, and baby brother, Waah.

Hetty's Yeti-shack was perched at the very edge of Mythica, Kingdom of Magical Creatures.

EQUILAND →

YETI-SHACK →

SMOKY HOLLOW ↑

MYTHICA SCHOOL →

SPARKLING LAKE →

ORACLE TEMPLE ↑

UNICORN PALACE ↓

MERVILLE →

POOL OF FEARS

FIRE MOUNTAIN

TROLL PEAK

CYCLOPSIA

ORGONSTONE

SIRENS

5

Chapter Two

One morning Hetty woke
up and knew something
was wrong.

Usually, baby Waah woke
her with his wailing ...

... sucking

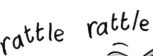

... or rattling!

But today he was quiet. Very quiet.

Hetty rushed over to baby
Waah's crib.

It was empty!

"Oh no!" she cried, dashing in to
Yeti-Mum and Yeti-Dad.

Someone's stolen the baby!

Ssshh Hetty. You'll wake little Waah!

Then she saw him, lying all tiny and pale between Yeti-Mum and Yeti-Dad.

"Nothing seems to make him better," whispered Yeti-Mum.

"Not the *Oracle*!" cried Hetty.
The Oracle was scary.
The Oracle talked in riddles.

"It's our only hope," sighed Yeti-Dad,
kissing them all goodbye. Then
he gave a loud Yeti-roar and
set off for work.

The Oracle lived in a very large temple just behind the Sparkling Lake. Hetty didn't want to go in.

"Have you brought a gift for the Oracle?" asked the sharp-eyed Harpy at reception.

"I suppose it will do," she sniffed, and let them pass through to the Oracle's mystic chamber.

The Oracle started to ripple and swirl. Then whispered words began tumbling around the room.

Gradually the words collected
into an echoing chant ...

Through fire, where icy peaks surround
The black and writhing Pool of Fears,
One sparkling sightless eye is found
To be crushed and swirled in healing tears.
Five hearts as one in friendship save
Infant son from early grave.

The glowing Oracle faded
to shadow, but the words
continued to whisper ...

Oh Yeti-Mum,
what do they
mean?

Suddenly the Harpy swooped
towards them.

Time's up!

"But we need to
take the words home,"
wailed Hetty.

I'll pay for
them with
honey-berries.

"Very well," rasped the Harpy, taking
a long slow breath.

15

All the air in the room began
swirling towards the Harpy,
as she sucked in the words …

eye…
sightless…
tears

… until there was no sound left.

Then she blew the words out into
a glittering jar, and stoppered it.

Release the stopper,
Release the words,
Return the stopper,
Return the words.

Finally the Harpy snatched the honey-
berries, and pushed the Yetis outside.

Chapter Three

Hetty and Yeti-Mum stood by the Sparkling Lake in despair. Hetty's friend, Molly, spotted them and came swimming over.

18

Yeti-Mum looked from Hetty to baby
Waah, and at last she handed over the
precious jar.

"True!" admitted Hetty. "But Jojo isn't! Let's go and find him!"

"I suppose so," sighed Molly.

Prince Jojo, the unicorn, was playing with his friend, Dingle Dragon. Hetty opened the jar, and they all listened hard to the Oracle's words.

...infant son from early grave

"Hmm … I think the infant son must be baby Waah," said Jojo, "but I haven't a clue what the rest means!"

Can't you use a spell to make the cure clearer?

Much too hard!

"We need Peg's brains, but he lives up in Equiland with the Deep Thinkers."

"Let's go!" whooped Dingle, flapping his wings excitedly.

Chapter Four

Jojo's magical wings didn't fly quite as fast as Dingle's, but soon they all arrived in Equiland.

Hi, Peg.

Peg sat listening to the Oracle's words, deep in thought, for ages.

...one sparkling Sightless eye...

At last, he replaced the stopper in the jar, and sighed deeply.

Can't you work it out either?

I can, but you'll soon wish I couldn't!

"You see," Peg went on, "the sparkling Sightless Eye is a rare pearl, that is found in just one place ... the Pool of Fears!"

So, let's get going!

Peg opened the Oracle's
jar once more.

Five hearts as one in friendship save
Infant son from early grave.

Molly, Dingle, Jojo, Peg and me —
that makes **five**... It's **our**
job to save baby Waah-gulp!

"Right," said Dingle. "We'd better get
going, then!"

Chapter Five

They flew all night across some of the most scary parts of Mythica.

At last, they landed at the edge of the Pool of Fears.

Suddenly, the glassy dark water started to move – *towards them*!

"M-m-me?" gulped Molly. "But how will you distract her? Look at all those heads!"

"We'll just have to use all our powers."

Hetty had a nasty feeling that their powers wouldn't be strong enough. Then she thought of poor baby Waah, and in her biggest, bravest voice, called down to the horrible heads below.

"Jojo, quick – do a magic trick or something," whispered Hetty urgently.

Jojo's eyes opened wide with dismay.

Jojo moved forward, and the Hydra heads swayed towards him. Then he started to spin airy threads of colour.

But only half the Hydra heads were watching Jojo's rainbows.

"We have to distract *all* the heads," whispered Peg. "I'll try a riddle!"

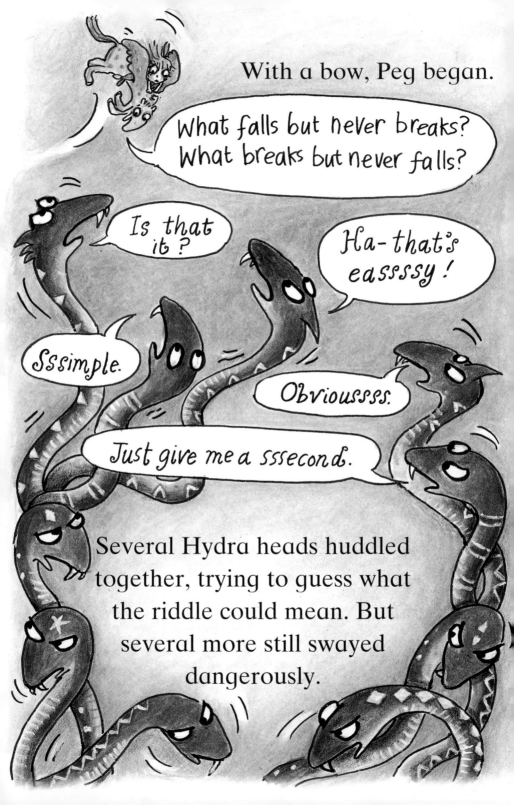

"Firework time!" breathed Dingle.

His fiery dragon breath made a wonderful display, especially when Jojo added a sprinkling of unicorn magic.

But four sets of Hydra eyes still guarded the water suspiciously.

Nervously, Molly began to sing. She watched in amazement as, one by one, the Hydra heads drooped, and every eye closed.

"Right," whispered Peg. "You've got to go *now*, Molly!"

"I'm going, too!" said Hetty, suddenly. "Jojo, can you make a spell to help me breathe underwater?"

Jojo waved his horn, and little sparks shimmered on Hetty's shoulders.

"Thanks, Jojo," she whispered, looking down into the icy black water. "Molly, are you ready?"

Molly nodded. Hetty took her hand and, together, they dived in.

Chapter Six

Hetty and Molly had
no idea what they were
searching for.

In fact, they should have wondered how
long the mermaid lullaby would last.

As the Hydra woke up, its coils started to writhe and thrash, and Molly and Hetty were blasted right across the lake floor.

Aagh!

Ouch!

Molly's fingers were caught in the jaws of an enormous shell. Horrified, Hetty struggled to heave it apart, using every bit of her Yeti-strength.

At last, the shell sprang open.

The S-S-Sightless Eye!

Hetty grabbed the pearl, but suddenly, her whole body started to shudder.

Desperately, Molly dragged her friend up through the water towards the surface. They'd done it!

Molly looked around.

They were surrounded by angry, hissing Hydra heads.

Dingle, Jojo and Peg came to the rescue.
They darted round the writhing heads,
shouting ...

... until the Hydra heads were in such a
muddle that Dingle and Peg could
swoop down and collect
Hetty and Molly.

The friends waved
a cheeky goodbye,
and began their
journey home.

Chapter Seven

"I hope we're in time!" panted Hetty, as they flew towards the Yeti-shack.

All their parents had gathered, and were wild with worry.

Hetty struggled out of her father's tight grasp and held up the pearl.

"The Sightless Eye!" murmured Peg's dad.

Hetty fumbled for the Oracle's jar, and released the lid.

"But I still don't understand the Oracle's words," sobbed Yeti-Mum.

Peg's dad rushed forward and collected her tears in the Oracle's jar. Then he crushed the pearl gently between his front hooves.

The sparkling dust streamed into the jar. The mixture shimmered and swirled.

Now baby waah must drink.

Baby Waah was barely breathing. Yeti-Mum carefully dropped some of the liquid into his mouth.

After a moment, the Yeti-baby coughed, opened his eyes, and looked around.

When he saw all the visitors, he waved his arms happily!

The party lasted for days.

But Hetty, Molly, Jojo, Dingle and Peg hardly noticed.

Psst-The answer to Peg's riddle is: Night and Day!